W.W. Denslow — *Denslow's Mother Goose*, 1901

Humpty-Dumpty sat on a wall,

Humpty-Dumpty had a great fall;

All the king's horses, and all

the king's men

Cannot put Humpty-Dumpty

together again.

(An egg)

W.W. Denslow — *Denslow's Mother Goose*, 1901

HUMPTY DUMPTY

A PICTORIAL HISTORY
BY
GEORGE W. B. SHANNON

Paul Woodroffe — *Thirty Old-time Nursery Songs*, ca. 1920

A STAR & ELEPHANT BOOK
THE GREEN TIGER PRESS

Text copyright © 1980 by George W.B. Shannon

ISBN 0-914676-37-7

A Star & Elephant Book
from
The Green Tiger Press
Box 868
La Jolla, California 92038

Color separation by Color Graphics, San Diego, California

Text set in Caslon 76
by Kaye and Farnsley, San Diego, California

Printing by The Green Tiger Press , San Diego, California

ACKNOWLEDGEMENTS

We wish to thank the following publishers for permission to use
material originally published by them: From *Rimes de la Mere Oie*
by Ormonde de Kay, Jr. Illustrations Copyright © 1971 by Push Pin
Studios, Inc., by permission of Little, Brown and Co. From *Borgmaster Munte* by Elsa Beskow. Copyright © Albert Bonniers For-
lag, Stockholm, 1965. For the illustration "Things" from *Ding Dong
Bell* by Edward Ardizzone Copyright © by the Edward Ardizzone
Estate, 1957. First published by Dennis Dobson Ltd, 1957. Permis-
sion granted by the Edward Ardizzone Estate. From *Sing Mother
Goose* by Opal Wheeler, illustrated by Marjorie Torrey. Copyright,
1945, by E.P. Dutton & Co., Inc. and reprinted by permission of the
Publisher. From *Tall Book of Mother Goose* illustrated by Feodor
Rojankovsky. Copyright 1942 by Western Publishing Company,
Inc. and used with their permission. Illustration reprinted from
Mother Goose Rhymes, pictures by Pablo Ramirez. Reprinted by
permission of William Collins Publishers. Copyright © 1966. From
Mother Goose: Seventy Seven Verses by Tasha Tudor, Copyright

Milton Glaser (Push Pin Studios) — *Rimes de la Mere Oie*, 1971

To my family.

Special thanks to

Margaret Coughlin
and
Anne McConnell

Paul Woodroffe — *Humpty Dumpty and Other Songs*, 1920

HUMPTY-DUMPTY

Riddles are found around the world and like the people who share them they are logical, illogical and filled with a sense of play and mystery. One of the most popular in English is the riddle-rhyme Humpty Dumpty, like most, so old that no one can be certain of when it was new. The rhyme is a puzzle in itself. There are hundreds of riddles describing eggs, yet it is Humpty Dumpty that has long been best known in English. It is also the only egg riddle to be adopted by the nebulous collection known as Mother Goose.

Part of its popularity must be attributed to the political overtones that have become so much a part of the riddle. To most adults, Humpty Dumpty is not only a riddle, but an ironic view of political ambition and its consequences. The leaders' power may have been absolute, but so is their fall.

Still, without any political overtones, Humpty Dumpty is more attractive than most egg riddles for it is a complete story as well as puzzle. It would not be possible to base an entire picturebook, as has often been done with Humpty, on "I threw it up as white as snow; like gold on a flag it fell below," one version of an egg riddle. Humpty Dumpty has been endowed with human characteristics over the years through illustration.

H for poor Humpty who after his fall. Felt obliged to resign his seat on the wall.

He is involved in a very brief intense plot that awakens one's empathy. As do most elements of folk literature that survive and thrive, Humpty Dumpty has universal appeal.

While it is accepted by all that the answer to the riddle is an egg, there are several theories as to what a Humpty Dumpty really was. Why was Humpty Dumpty used for the comparison? Both Katherine Elwes Thomas (*The Real Personages of Mother Goose*) and Albert Stevens (*The Nursery Rhyme: Remnant of Popular Protest*) believe that the riddle began as a political lampoon toward King Richard III (1452-1485). If so, it would make Humpty about the same age as Christopher Columbus.

As the king's men were at hand, though unable to repair, Stevens suggests that the scene of the riddle is a battle field. His explanation is further supported by his documented translation from past English usage of "sate on a wall" to "attacked a Welshman." It was

Walter Crane
— *Walter Crane's Absurd ABC*, 1874

L. Leslie Brooke
— *The Nursery Rhyme Book*, 1897

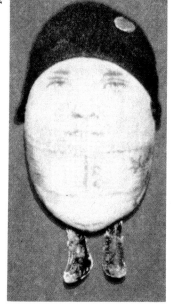

'Napoleon' Humpty Dumpty,
hand-sewn of velvet, ca. 1820.
Courtesy of the Atlanta Toy Museum.

during the War of the Roses while fighting the Welsh that the humpbacked Richard III was killed in battle.

It is this analogy to King Richard that lends itself to the contemporary cartoons of fallen unpopular leaders. Cartoons such as the October 8, 1973 cover of *Newsweek* (Spiro Agnew) maintain the lampoon qualities of the riddle and do as much for keeping the riddle alive as all the nursery rhyme collections.

A less popular interpretation is that the rhyme actually concerns a primitive war tank — a type of Trojan Turtle — that was to cross a river and attack the enemies of Charles I (1600-1649). The secret attack, however, was discovered and the river widened by the enemy. Upon attack the tank (soon named Humpty Dumpty for unknown reasons by both sides) sank, killing many of the king's men inside. As support for this interpretation Jean Harrowven in *The Origins of Rhymes, Songs and Sayings* quotes a lesser known variant of the riddle-rhyme:

Humpty Dumpty lay in the beck, (a small brook)
With all his sinews around his neck;
All the king's surgeons, and all the king's wrights,
   (builders)
Could not put Humpty Dumpty to rights.[1]

It is impossible to determine which if either of the accounts is accurate; or if it is of any consequence. Perhaps both are correct as the people molded the folk rhyme to suit their needs. An interesting adaptation of the name was the seventeenth century drink known as a Humpty Dumpty made of ale boiled in brandy that left one not likely to rise too soon after falling.[2] Out of this definition grew the derogatory adjective, Humpty Dumpty, as used in 1699 by Richard Bently in his printed attack on William King as a "Humpty-Dumpty Author."[3] Time has greatly changed the image of Humpty Dumpty, and he is known by most today as a friendly nursery character.

Most people in the U.S. and England know the egg creature in the riddle as Humpty Dumpty, yet as soldiers and emigrants moved about the world he gathered a long list of aliases and variations. Nova Scotians tell of: Roly-poly 'gin the wall,/ Roly-poly had a great fall,/ Ten score men and ten score more/ Couldn't put the roly-poly back as it was before.[4] Those of Barbados speak of Hoity Doity: Hoity Doity sat on a wall,/ Hoity Doity got a fall,/ Not the strongest man in town/ Couldn't put back Hoity Doity on the wall.[5] One of the few sex identified characters is found in the Blue Ridge Mountains as: Humpy on a wall/ Humpy Bumpy got a fall/ Ten men, ten more,/ Can't fix Humpy Bumpy/ The way she was before.[6]

Few of the variants include any king's men. Instead, Humpty et al are tended by equally helpless doctors and laymen. In at least two English variations there are neither king's men nor a fall:

Humpty Dumpty went to town
Humpty Dumpty tore his gown;
All the needles in the town
Couldn't mend Humpty Dumpty's gown.

Humpty Dumpty and his brother
Were as like as one another,
Couldn't tell one from t'other
Humpty Dumpty and his brother.[7]

How Humpty Dumpty, the King's Favorite, sat upon a wall.

How the same Humpty Dumpty Fell off the wall.

How the King

From The *Pictorial Humpty Dumpty*, 1843. Illustrations reproduced by permission of the Houghton Library, Harvard University.

Lilla Måns Klumpedump satt uti ett trä;
och Klumpedumpen trilla ner och slog sitt lilla knä.
Och kungens alla hästar och kungens alla män,
de kunde inte oraga upp MånsKlumpedump igen.

Elsa Beskow — *Borgmaster Munte*, 1922

In Germany Humpty is known as Humpelken-Pumpelken, Gigele-Gagle and Etje-Paetje among others. The French monikers include Boule-Boule, while he is Lille Trille (Little Fall Down) or the like in Scandinavia.[8] An element leading support to the theory that the rhyme migrated rather than being native to all areas is found in the fact that an early French variation refers to England:

Boule, boule su l'keyer
Boule, boule par terre
Y n'a nuz homme en Angleterre
Pou e'erfaire.[9]

Ball ball on the wall
Ball ball on the ground
No man in England can be found
Who can mend the fallen ball.

Publishing has increased the travels of the egg creature as well. As a result, Humpty Dumpty has been translated into languages as diverse as Hebrew, Russian and Japanese.

While Humpty Dumpty is found in most contemporary editions of Mother Goose, its oral tradition kept it out of the earliest printings. The most notable exclusion was Oliver Goldsmith's *Mother Goose's Melodies* (the first edition of any distinction) published by John Newbery around 1765. The riddle's earliest known recording is hand written as an addition to an 1803 copy of the same title.[10] Humpty was not "legitimized" by print until 1810 and then in *Gammer Gurton's Garland: or The Nursery Parnassus: A Choice Collec-*

tion of Pretty Songs and Verses, For The Amusement of All Little-Good Children Who Can Neither Read Nor Run,[11] a title longer than the riddle itself. In its printed debut Humpty Dumpty appeared as:

Humpty-Dumpty sate on a wall,
Humpty-Dumpty had a great fall;
Threescore men and threescore more
Cannot place Humpty-Dumpty as he was before.

As publishing and technology improved, new editions of Mother Goose appeared throughout the 19th century. Year after year, old editions went out of print as new ones were published. This, combined with the way children literally "use to pieces" their favorite books accounts for the few surviving early illustrations. They simply vanished. It is known that early in the 1800's Humpty was becoming one of the "stars" of Mother Goose and was published as a single book in several instances.[12] By 1842 the riddle-rhyme had changed somewhat and added "all the king's men," the line later used in book titles dealing with politics such as *All The King's Men* by Warren and *All The President's Men* by Woodward and Bernstein:

Humpty Dumpty sate on a wall,
Humpty Dumpty had a great fall;
All the king's soldiers and all the king's men
Cannot set Humpty Dumpty up again.[13]

A year later, 1843, Humpty Dumpty appeared in the hand colored *Pictorial Humpty Dumpty* published in London. Designed more as a panorama or Japanese folding book it measured 9 x 23 cm. when closed and grew to a full 159 cm. when unfolded. The verse was printed in English and French on the front and had six translations on the back side. In this version, Humpty's fall seems to have been precipitated by an overindulgence in drinking and the suspense was increased as the king's men attempted to hoist the fallen Favorite back to the top of the wall:

How Humpty Dumpty, the King's Favorite,
   sat upon a wall
How the same Humpty Dumpty fell off the wall
How the King, having heard of his Favorite's misfortune
ordered out all his horses and all his men,
repaired to the spot and superintended in person
the raising of the prostrate Humpty Dumpty.
How the King's attempt to raise his Favorite failed.
How the weight of Humpty Dumpty was so great
that he dragged forward many of the King's men,
and how the rope breaking, all the rest
for many miles fell backwards.

Most recent editions have used a streamlined variation with a shorter last line and dropped the "e" on sate. The last line change may be due to Alice in *Through The Looking Glass*, who, while visiting with Humpty Dumpty, commented, "That last line is much too long for the poetry."[14]

While Lewis Carroll featured Humpty in a chapter all his own and assigned him the task of "translating" *The Jabberwocky*, James Joyce went even further. In *Finnegan's Wake* Joyce used Humpty Dumpty as "one of the book's basic symbols; the great cosmic egg whose

18

fall like that of the drunken Finnegan, suggests the fall of Lucifer and the fall of man."[15] Others, less ambitious, have written sonnets, eulogies and plain doggerel about the egg creature that began as a riddle.

Thomas Walsh's sonnet (circa 1928) interestingly refers to three related yet varying interpretations of Humpty used by illustrators earlier in the century:

Clown-monarch of the nursery, thy name
  Too long is silent on the sonnet's tongue,
  The while our bards sophisticate have sung
Thy cousin Pierrot and his deeds to fame!
Is't air of carnival thou lackst?—a dame,
  Like Columbine, to interest the young
  With that "love-interest" that is set among
The chief requirements of the author's game?

Kings prove, they say, their greatness in their fall,
  So thou, mad bumpking from the moon, has shown
  Thy merriment to childish eyes alone
That hail thy tumble as a royal flight—
Little barbarians, with no thought at all
To sympathize, or keep a face polite.[16]

Other writers have found it their duty to expand or rewrite the rhyme, particularly at the turn of the century. L. Frank Baum of Oz fame in his *Mother Goose in Prose* (1897/1901) opens his tale with the birth of Humpty and writes of his brothers and sisters all waiting to hatch. In a fight for more room in the nest Humpty gets the heave-ho and is soon on his adventures. Found by a princess, she helps him up on a wall so as to watch the king and all his men parade by. In his excitement Humpty falls, yet "even in his death, Humpty did repay the kindness of the fair girl who had shown him such sights as an egg seldom sees."[17] He becomes the source of the riddle used by the prince to win the hand of the princess. The core element — the accident — of Baum's prose rhyme finds a very similar representation in Leslie Brooke's 1922 six page visualization of the rhyme.

Oliver Booth for *Old Nursery Rhymes Dug Up at the Pyramids* (1903?) "dug up" the following four stanzas:

Alice in Wonderland, with W.C. Fields as Humpty Dumpty, 1933

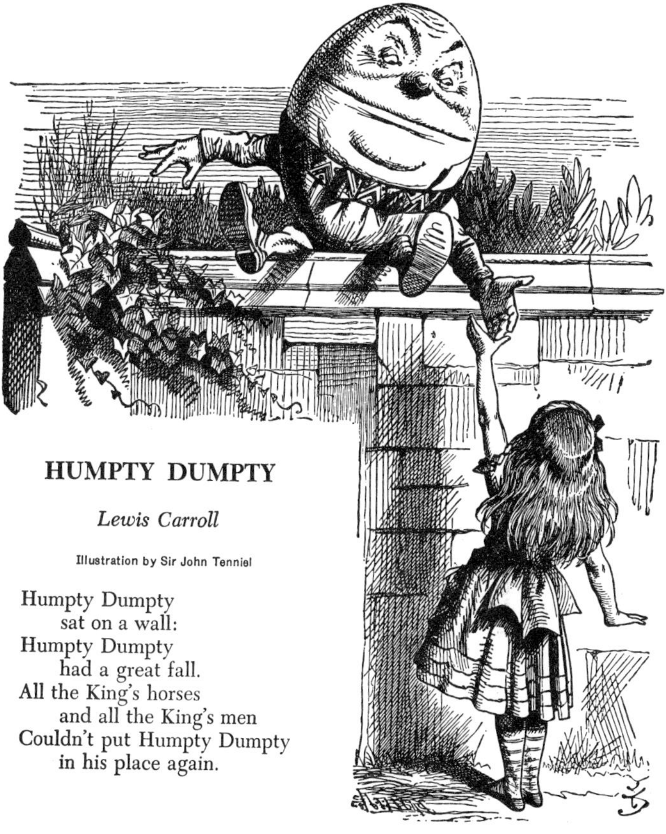

HUMPTY DUMPTY

Lewis Carroll

Illustration by Sir John Tenniel

Humpty Dumpty
    sat on a wall:
Humpty Dumpty
    had a great fall.
All the King's horses
    and all the King's men
Couldn't put Humpty Dumpty
    in his place again.

John Tenniel — *Through the Looking Glass*, 1872

Humpty-Dumpty, fragile and round,
Certainly chose a position unsound.
When he elected to sit on a wall,
His neighbors all told him he surely would fall.

They cackled and quacked, "Your neck you'll break,"
Two of them gave him a push and a shake;
But still he sat there, "Don't worry," he said,
"I can't break my neck, for you see I'm all head."

Obstinate Humpty fell with a crash,
Spectators say 'twas a terrible smash;
The news, as did Humpty, quickly spread,
"We told you so," then the neighbors said.

Humpty-Dumpty early next day,
Was wanted at breakfast-time, they say;
The youth who sought said, at that sight,
"I wish I'd have had him for supper last night."[18]

Anna Marion Smith created a slightly more didactic
and perhaps political extension for *St. Nicholas* in
1907:

There he lay, stretched out on the ground,
While all the company gathered around;
When, valiantly stifling his tears and his groans,
He sadly addressed them in quavering tones.

"Friends," said Humpty, wiping his eyes,
"This sudden descent was an awful surprise.
It inclines me to think—you may laugh at my views,—
That a seat that is humble is safest to choose."

"All are not fitted to sit on a wall,
Some have no balance, and some are too small;

Many have tried it and found, as I guess,
They've ended, like me, in a terrible mess."

"Hark, you horses, and all you king's men!
Hear it, and never forget it again!
'T is those who are patient in seats that are low,
Who some day get up in high places and crow."

Then they took him and put him to bed.
I hope you'll remember the things that he said;
For all the king's horses and all the king's men
Never once thought of his sermon again.[19]

The most curious alterations have been to modernize
and personalize Humpty's plight while maintaining
the fuel of the nursery rhyme. George Chappel in
Mother's Geese (1906) gave Humpty Dumpty a car
with:

Humpty Dumpty flew at a hill
Humpty Dumpty had a fine spill,
All things, horse-power
and chassis so stout
Couldn't help Humpty Dumpty
When Humpty Dumped out.[20]

Fanny Cory — *The Fanny Cory Mother Goose*, 1913

Humpty Dumpty sat on a wall.
Humpty Dumpty had a great fall.
All the King's horses and all the
                                    King's men
Couldn't put Humpty Dumpty
            together again."

81-228

I

There he lay, stretched out on the ground,
While all the company gathered around;
When, valiantly stifling his tears and his
    groans,
He sadly addressed them in quavering tones.

II

"Friends," said Humpty, wiping his eyes,
"This sudden descent was an awful surprise.
It inclines me to think,—you may laugh at
    my views,—
That a seat that is humble is safest to choose.

Anna Marion Smith — *St. Nicholas*, January 1907

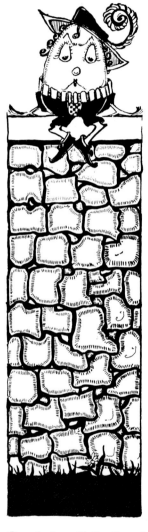

Science also had its turn in 1971 with Dr. Earle Hackett's

Humpty Dumpty sat on a wall
Humpty Dumpty had a great fall.
It's the same for an egg
As for eggshell ceramics
You can't beat the Second Law
of Thermodynamics.[21]

With time, Humpty will surely be falling from space ships and foreign planets.

Grace Irwin — *Mother Goose in Song and Rhyme*, 1930

PICTURES

Edward Ardizzone — *Ding Dong Bell*, 1957

To illustrate a riddle is to literally reveal the answer, yet Humpty Dumpty has been drawn by hundreds of illustrators. While the riddle's answer is an egg, illustrators have done far more than draw plain white eggs. Taking their cues from the historical background of the riddle, the story, and its nursery popularity, illustrators have a broad range of possibilities from which to choose. Depending on his interests, talent and politics the artist may either literalize the rhyme by depicting one of the historical theories explaining the riddle, expand it into something new, or make it saccharine. It is in the weakest editions of Mother Goose where Humpty Dumpty appears so cuddly soft and severely cute that he could not possibly break.

Most illustrators have chosen the more literal format, drawing a mutant egg/man of royalty or the upper class: a personage of enough importance to receive the aid of all the king's men. By way of costume Humpty Dumpty has belonged to numerous branches of the mil-

Marjorie Torrey — *Sing Mother Goose*, 1945

itary and has worn everything from frilly leotards to a pin-striped business suit. These last two extremes were both drawn to depict a French or classical European Humpty Dumpty.

H. Willebeek Le Mair (1911), a Dutch artist who studied with the picture book master Boutet de Monvel sets her egg/man in an elaborately designed past. Her oval illustrations define a sense of courtliness and refinement with their soft pastels. Indeed, her mirrored ovals resemble one of Faberge's famous jeweled eggs of the same period — an egg cut open to reveal the story inside. This Humpty Dumpty in his leotards and ruffle is certainly a cousin to the French clown/mime Pierrot mentioned in the verse by Thomas Walsh.

Barbara Cooney's 1964 illustration is as much of Wall Street as the Left Bank. Hers is an urbane Humpty in double breasted suit and of an unknown distinguished career. Why a businessman would choose smilingly to straddle a stone wall is anyone's guess. The absurdity of the situation invites the resulting calamity.

Maxfield Parrish produced two of the most aristocratic eggs over a twenty-four year period. His 1897 illustration for Baum's *Mother Goose In Prose* in black and white is complete with devilish eye and dashing curl on his forehead. He is not an inviting creature — appearing rather aloof and conceited. He is a classic case of pride goeth before the fall. This was Parrish's first book illustration assignment and was quite popular. In 1900 each chapter of the book was printed separately and offered as a premium to users of Pettijohns Breakfast Food.[22]

Arthur Rackham's 1913 pen and ink Humpty Dumpty in contrast invites empathy. There is the nervous look of Edward Everett Horton rather than the air of the elite. The nattily dressed Humpty appears fearful of the troops marching behind him.

Parrish brought Humpty back in 1921 for an Easter cover of *Life*. This time out Humpty was in full color and strictly British with tea cup and Eaton collar. Another thoroughly British egg was served up by Seiichi Horiuchi in the 1975 Japanese edition of Mother Goose. Except for the illustrations moving from right to left, all appears to be happening in downtown London with double decker buses and English ads for gin and monster movies. With his cigar and top hat Humpty bears more than a passing resemblence to Churchill. As the most admired models in Japan are Occidental it is not surprising that Paris based Horiuchi's Anglo Mother Goose was a bestseller. It is still possible that an Asian Humpty Dumpty exists (perhaps a kimono clad egg). Though such illustrations are lost to the West, the first Japanese translation of Mother Goose occurred between 1914 and 1926 before the overwhelming influence of the West.[23]

Two other decidedly English Humpty Dumptys were drawn by Raymond Briggs of England for his *Ring-a-Ring o' Roses* (1962) and *The Mother Goose Treasury* (1966 and Greenaway Medal winner). Both with top hat and umbrella look as if they stopped off to rest on the wall in route to parliament. Briggs' color and design are (perhaps appropriately) as proper and stiff as a British upper lip — yet another visualization of pride before the fall.

If the fall is to be humorous (and it must if it is to maintain the lampoon quality) it is important that Humpty *not* be a sympathetic individual. The more pompous Humpty Dumpty's image the more humorous and perhaps deserved his fall. It is much funnier for most to see a wealthy snob fall on a banana peel than a gentle child.

The egg/men decked out in military finery must not only be pompous but visualize the enemy (for most) if they are to have any justification in falling to their deaths. Political lampoons are not created by one's allies, but by those who wish to see one defeated. The strongest example of this is Feodor Rojankovsky's "Hitler" Humpty Dumpty done a year after the artist fled the Nazi invasion of Paris.[24] At the time of its publication, 1942, it was only a hoped-for allegory. The details of his color illustrations extend the wish for Hitler's fall as a crow or raven, symbol of coming death, perches near Humpty, then flies off as he falls. Once he does fall Humpty's size is realized as gargantuan for his

Arthur Rackham — *Mother Goose: The Old Nursery Rhymes*, ca. 1913

broken shell is as big as the kings men's horses. Of all the illustrations, Rojankovsky's decidedly contemporary variation is the closest to the rhyme's political origins.

While the most popular historical explanation of Humpty is that he was a king, illustrations depicting Humpty as human rather than an egg/man tend to show him as a commoner or a bumpkin. The 1876 illustrations in *Mother Goose's Nursery Rhymes and Fairy Tales* by Sir John Gilbert and others cannot seem to make up its mind. The left page illustration depicts a man of wealth falling from the wall as an egg drops out of his hand. The facing illustration over the music is of a country boy either sleeping or moaning on top of the wall. While both illustrations are pen and ink, it is most likely that they were done by different illustrators as the design of the wall and difference in facial detail would indicate. An anonymous 1903 illustration published by Dutton in *Mother Goose's Nursery Rhymes* depicts a Humpty greatly similar to the characters of Stan Laurel and Ed Wynn that were not known until much later. A gentle bumpkin, waspish hair and a simple/kind smile fill Humpty's face as his fingers wiggle nervously.

Kate Greenaway pictures Humpty Dumpty as a puffy cheeked little boy in her 1881 illustration and omits the last two lines of the verse. It would be very difficult to destroy this innocent child with the traditional ending. Greenaway merely presents Humpty Dumpty who from the forlorn expression of his face, could have already experienced his "great fall" and be in the process of emotional recovery as the skinned knee stops hurting.

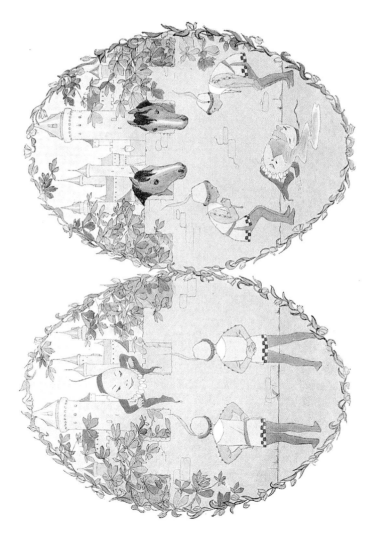

H. Willebeek Le Mair — *Our Old Nursery Rhymes*, 1911

It is Walter Crane's 1874 illustration for the letter "H" in his *Absurd ABC* that comes closest to actually picturing Richard III. At least it is Shakespeare's image of the king — a fallen hunchback with crown and sceptor at his feet. While Crane's brightly colored Humpty physically resembles Richard III, he does not perish. Instead he is helped to his feet by a well dressed gentleman.

Humpty Dumpty sat on a wall,
Humpty Dumpty had a great fall.

Kate Greenaway — *Mother Goose: Or The Old Nursery Rhymes*, 1881

Humpty Dumpty has fallen while battling rats, bees, birds, firecrackers and cannonballs. His greatest foes seem to be, however, gravity and fate — the perils of being alone at the top; or what or who goes up must come down. Fall he always does, yet not always from a wall.

Scandinavian illustrations for the riddle-rhyme have Humpty or, as he is known there in print, Klumpe Dumpe, forever falling out of trees whether he be egg/man, fool or royal child. Elsa Beskow's 1922 full color illustration depicts a royal child who as the text states fell from a tree (tra) and hurt his knee (kna). The need for a rhyme seems to have had as much to do with Klumpe's fate as anything else. The child evidently weighs a great deal for all the king's horses and all the king's men cannot pull him up again. Here the rhyme is

Elsa Beskow — *Borgmaster Munte*, 1922

no longer a riddle. A hurt knee has nothing to do with an egg or the inability to be put back together again.

The freckle faced stooge in pen and ink by Jorgen Clevin (1951) drawn for a Danish edition suffers little more than dizziness upon his crash. Resembling a cauliflower faced boxer, one is curious as to why the king's men are rushing to his aid.

The 1900 translation by Knud Rosentand kept the tree, but rephrased the line and offers a new rhyme of gren and sten. With this to work from Sigurd Wandel's illustration is a study in pending disaster. Balancing on a structurally impossible branch, a be-limbed egg sits smiling blissfully over a big stone. The slightest breeze would send this pen and ink Humpty beyond a point of repair.

Humpty is drawn as a bull-tossed toreador with no walls or king's men in sight as illustrated by Barbara Cooney (1968) for the Spanish translation of Mother Goose published in the U.S. Already stricken, this Humpty's demise seems certain as soon as he hits the ground in the arena.

Humpty Dumpty sat on a wall,
Humpty Dumpty had a great fall;

All the King's horses
and all the King's men

Cannot put Humpty Dumpty
together again.

Feodor Rojankovsky —
Tall Book of Mother Goose, 1942

While the rhyme of Humpty Dumpty has been adopted by the nursery the fact that its origins were adult and centered on death creates difficulties in its illustration. Most artists take the "safe" way out and illustrate Humpty only on the wall. Still, a few illustrate the fatal climax as well.

How does one kill a main character in a nursery rhyme? Some have eased the crash by creating a type of life after death. Broken anthropomorphic eggs leave anthropomorphic yolks and whites behind. W.W. Denslow produced two such Humpty's early in the century. Both depicted as clowns they were published in *Denslow's Mother Goose* (1901) and *Denslow's Humpty Dumpty and Other Stories* (1903). Upon crashing the first Humpty became a crying yolk-man complete with buttons. The second was saved from death by being hard boiled. Denslow felt a protectiveness toward children and said so, "I don't always adhere to the text of the familiar nursery rhymes. I believe in pure fun for the child, and I believe it can be given them

Maxfield Parrish — *Life Magazine* cover, 1921

without any incidental gruesomeness."[25] As he simplified the rhymes so he did his illustrations. His Humpty Dumptys are illustrated in heavy lines, simple forms and minimal flat colors.

A modern Russian edition of Mother Goose in primary colors offers some hope of recovery as the soldiers pick up the egg white with their spears and the yolk wearily smiles. Humpty appears a bit embarrassed for his lack of balance and may have learned his lesson.

Oompie Doompie as he is called in South Africa falls but only cracks in the 1957 Johannesburg pen and ink edition. Humpty appears to be repairable with little more than glue, but not as the translation dictates by herbs and spices:

Humpty Dumpty sat on the wall
Humpty Dumpty had a hard fall
Give him coriander
Or give him cinnamon
But that will never make him whole.[26]

Those illustrations foregoing "life beyond the fall" go past the lampoon qualities of the rhyme and replace the possible joviality with the macabre. The 1870 leotard and tunic dressed variation by the Brothers Dalziel is one of the most chilling illustrations. Humpty Dumpty is no longer "just" a decorated egg or fallen man. Save the running yolk, there is complete stillness in the illustration. He is clearly and painfully dead. His body lies limp and his egg/skull at an odd angle is broken open with its contents running like a stream across the ground. This Humpty dies alone with nothing but a large frog as witness.

Though he does not illustrate the crash, Frederick Richardson's 1915 illustration is one of the most intense. Shown in mid-fall his hands are grasping for the wall as his immense and fragile skull careens toward the stone walk below. The image of the final destruction seconds away is as strong as the actual illustration. Richardson's shimmering colors emphasize the violence of the crash.

A handful of illustrators have gone beyond the staid drawings of Humpty Dumpty and as with any interpretive venture some have met with greater success than others. Two chose to draw only eggs with sketched faces. Willy Pogany's 1928 pen and ink Humpty Dumpty has no chance for survival as he must try to balance on a slanted wall — an interesting interpretation on the verge of the market crash and depression. A Merlin-like wiseman and soldier stand puzzling over the cracks in Pablo Ramirez' 1966 giant egg that sits on

Pablo Ramirez — *Mother Goose Rhymes*, 1966

Humpty Dumpty sat on a wall.
Humpty Dumpty had a great fall;
All the king's horses and all the king's men
Couldn't put Humpty Dumpty together again.

Frederick Richardson — *Mother Goose*, 1901

W.W. Denslow — *Denslow's Mother Goose*, 1901

the floor as if a globe with a face. The dress of the soldier and the air of Merlin can but call to mind the popularity of Camelot in the early sixties both as a musical and as a political state of mind that ended suddenly with the death of President Kennedy.

Two of the more curious illustrations relate in turn to Egypt and Easter. While Oliver Booth stretched the rhyme into four stanzas, Stanley Adamson in *Nursery Rhymes Dug Up at the Pyramids* (1913?) created a monochromatic Egyptian combination of "King on the Mountain" and "Which came first — the chicken or the egg." Within borders which are parodies themselves, an egg creature with legs but no arms sits on the wall with a smile of supremacy. Large birds gather and soon kill it by knocking it off the wall at which time two fowl triumphantly take their place on the top of the wall. Though far from the rhyme's English origins there is one of the king's (or Pharaoh's) men on hand though, of course, unable to help. Gertrude Elliott's pinkish 1945 illustration combined the United States' fondness for both Easter and Humpty Dumpty. Here, Humpty is an Easter egg decorated as a rabbit. Again there is present the ill omen of a crow as well as three suspicious looking boys who either found or knocked down the giant Easter egg.

In two different editions Paul Woodroffe illustrated Humpty Dumpty as an egg/man enraptured in the joys of smoking a pipe. Woodroffe's 1920 drawing presents Humpty as a Jester puffing away as the king's men pass by in parade. While both illustrations seem to visually belong to the drug oriented 1960's rather than the first quarter of the century it is his color illustration (see title page) that is the most curious. Dressed à la the middle-east, this be-turbaned Humpty sits literally and figuratively wrapped-up in his water pipe and blissfully blowing smoke rings.

Charles Addams in *The Chas. Addams Mother Goose* (1967) chose to print only the first two lines of the rhyme as did Greenaway, but with drastically different illustrations. Addams' wall appears to be as high as the Empire State building. The angle of the black and white drawing shows "ant-sized" king's men looking up from below as an egg painted as a boy is perched on top of the wall. Upon crashing, the egg does not so much break as hatch for out pops a vicious-eyed and snaggle-toothed dragonette that frightens both king's men and their horses.

Tasha Tudor — *Mother Goose: Seventy Seven Verses*, 1944

Wallace Tripp — *Granfa' Grig Had a Pig & Other Rhymes*
Without Reason From Mother Goose, 1976

Beni Montressor — *I Saw a Ship-a-Sailing*, 1967

Many have illustrated the rhyme in editions set to music, but none have continued their illustrations into the music itself as did H.A. Rey in *Humpty Dumpty and Other Mother Goose Songs* (1943). Rey's Humpty is a bard-like egg balanced on a wall to perform. The music below is drawn in "egg-notation" with whole eggs being quarter notes and deviled eggs being eighth notes.

Thirty-three years later Wallace Tripp in *Grandfa' Grig Had a Pig and Other Rhymes Without Reason From Mother Goose* (1976) illustrated the rhyme with Humpty being only an egg. In three sequential color drawings an anonymous paw tosses the egg or Humpty over the wall where it lands on the king's head. It is curious that Tripp saw and illustrated this riddle with a long historical background as a "rhyme without reason."

If any illustrations reflect Harrowven's theory that Humpty was a war tank it is Montressor's 1967 drawing in *I Saw a Ship-a-Sailing*, a book dedicated to Frederico Fellini. A gigantic egg — a Trojan egg with

Douglas Hall — *Old Mother Goose in New Dress*, 1932

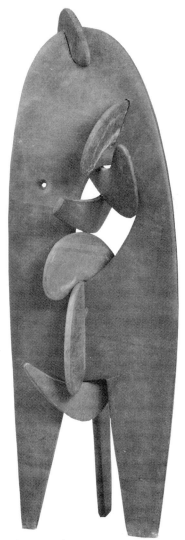

Isamu Noguchi — *Humpty Dumpty*, (1946.) Ribbon slate. 58¾ × 20¾ × 18 inches. Collection of the Whitney Museum of American Art.

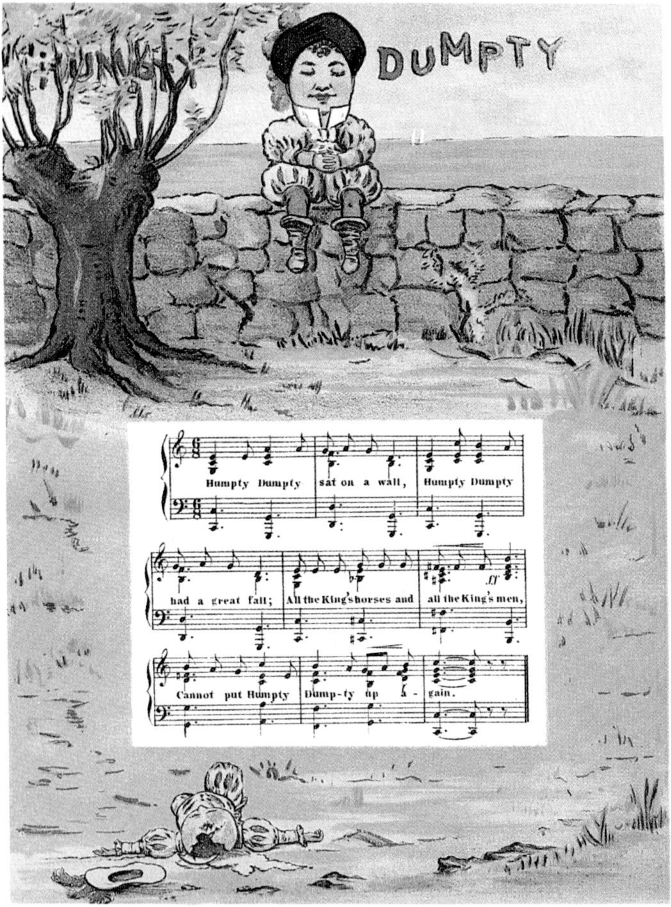
DUMPTY
Humpty Dumpty sat on a wall, Humpty Dumpty
had a great fall; All the King's horses and all the King's men,
Cannot put Humpty Dump-ty up a-gain.

J.L. Webb — *Mother Goose*, 1888

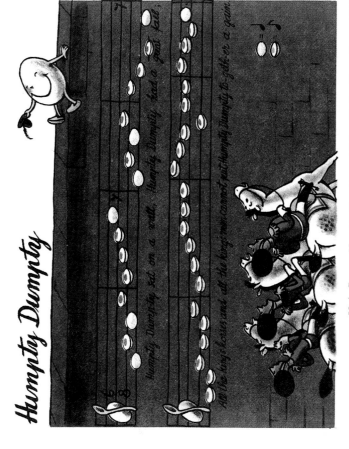

H.A. Rey — *Humpty Dumpty and Other Mother Goose Songs*, 1943

chick-disguised children inside — has broken outside the palace walls. As he watches, all the king's men are working to set it right. The bold flat colors and pen and ink drawings show Montressor's sense of staging and his study of cinema. Whether or not he was aware of the tank theory, it is interesting that Montressor should produce such a Trojan egg during the heavy fighting in Southeast Asia. His reason for doing the book was that "No one took care of the craziness in Mother Goose, the color, the magic of the poems and of their music."[27]

Douglas Hall's Humpty Dumpty in *Old Mother Goose In New Dress* (1932) is in very different dress indeed. Appearing as a toy egg with four spider-like legs he falls or rather disassembles so neatly that any self-respecting child could put him back together again. He is more a toy than an egg. The fate of Hall's Humpty Dumpty is similar to that of Isamu Noguchi's five foot slate sculpture entitled "Humpty Dumpty," (1945). During a crowded exhibition at the Whitney Museum a child pushed forward to touch the sculpture at which point the abstract creation came crashing to the ground — some section shattering to bits. When told, Noguchi laughed at the coincidence of the accident and the sculpture.[28]

Of all the illustrative interpretations and expansions, none has developed Humpty Dumpty's existence as fully as did L. Leslie Brooke in *Ring o' Roses* (1922). In treating the rhyme as the short story it is, Brooke created five illustrations over six pages that give Humpty personality and life. He is one of the few with any reason to be on the wall. Humpty is seen climbing to the top of the wall and waving his handkerchief on a stick. This commoner of an egg/man is filled with joy — the joy of the king's parade passing by. Excitement leads to carelessness and down he falls (on a double spread full color page) with only two child servants showing any alarm. Having littered the king's path his men, of course, seek to remedy the situation. But Humpty is far beyond repair and so is buried at the sight of his demise. While all Humpty Dumptys must die, Brooke was perhaps the first to allow this child-hood favorite the same ritual all children give the things they love which die, be they toy or pet — a grave marker. Brooke's Humpty Dumpty displays the child in everyone and his fall is all the sadder for it is in no way deserved. Few have shown such concern or respect for the riddle/rhyme *and* offered an extended interpretation. Brooke created an entirely new story without altering any of the words. His two sets of illustrations for Humpty Dumpty (these and a traditional one done in 1987) are true illustrative homonyms — the same words with two completely different meanings. To "read" Brooke's 1922 Humpty Dumpty is much like hearing a familiar poem or piece of music performed by a fine artist. One recognizes the work, but feels he has never really heard it before.

With its numerous histories and mysteries, Humpty Dumpty will continue to be a rich source of illustrations with more new interpretations always possible. The combined qualities of evolving folklore, adventure story and puzzle assure the verse and character a long life.

Humpty Dumpty sat on a wall,
Humpty Dumpty had a great fall;
All the king's horses and all the king's men
Couldn't put Humpty together again.

Alice and Martin Provenson — *The Mother Goose Book*, 1976

Nicola Bayley — *Nicola Bayley's Book of Nursery Rhymes*, 1975

HUMPTY DUMPTY.

H UMPTY DUMPTY sat on a wall;

Humpty Dumpty had a great fall ;

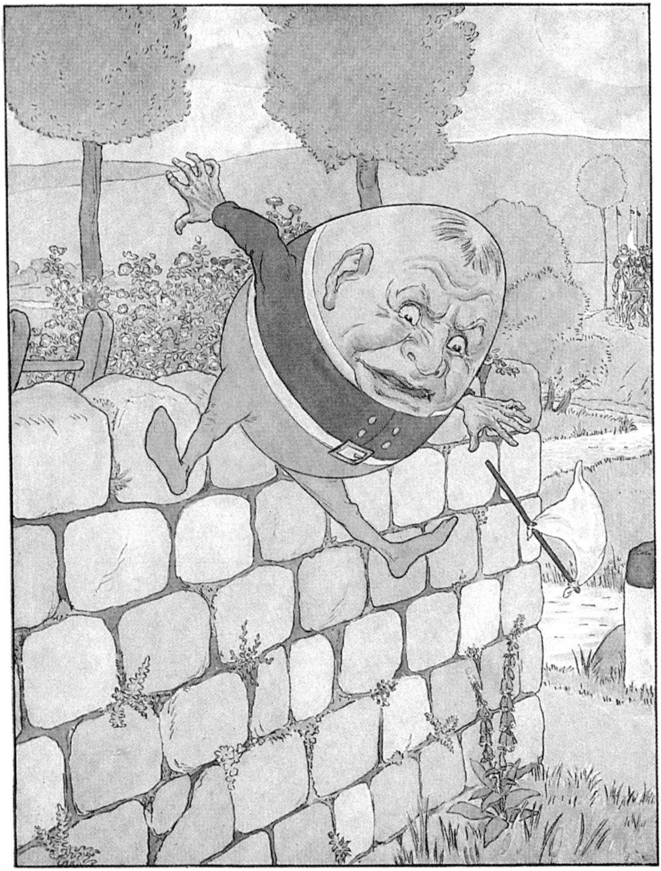

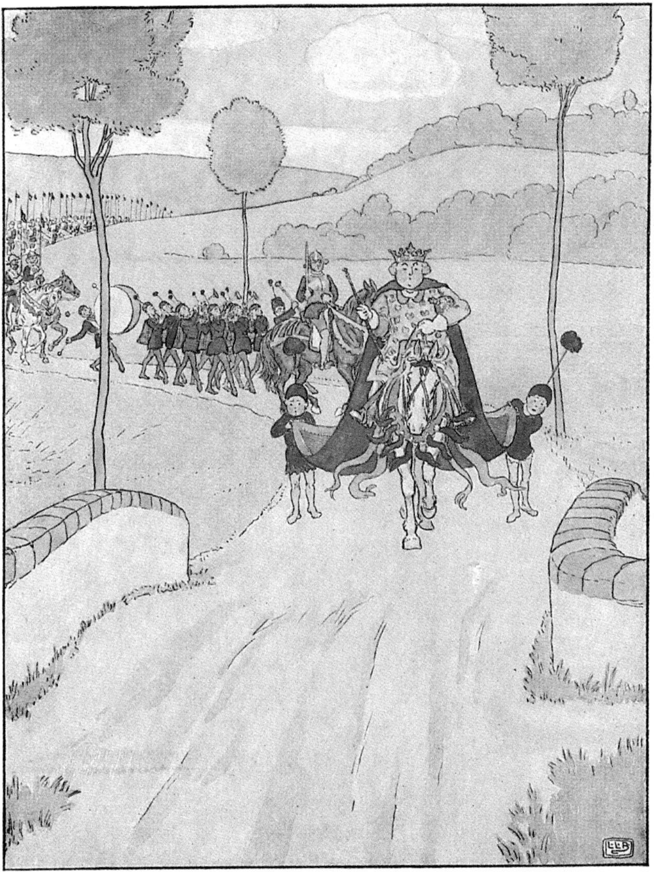

All the King's horses and all the King's men
Couldn't put Humpty Dumpty together again.

Here fell
Humpty
Dumpty

L. Leslie Brooke — *Ring O' Roses* and *Oranges and Lemons*,
 ca. 1900

Milo Winter — *Through the Looking Glass*, n.d.

"You seem very clever at explaining words, Sir," said Alice. "Would you kindly tell me the meaning of the poem 'Jabberwocky'?"

"Let's hear it," said Humpty Dumpty. "I can explain all the poems that ever were invented — and a good many that haven't been invented just yet."

— *Alice Through the Looking Glass*

Jane Breskin Zalben — *Jabberwocky*, 1977

Humpty Dumpty was nobody's fool
Even though it is a classic tale
How he knew nothing to begin with,
Learned nothing, came to nothing.—
An egg, sitting on a wall, they tell it.—
And he took a tumble and they could never
Put the pieces of him together again.

Whether he was a good egg or a bad egg,
Whether he was inspected, approved, passed,
Whether he was scrub or thoroughbred,
The record says nobody knows
And if they did they wouldn't tell.

Whether he climbed up the wall by himself,
Whether somebody else put him up on the wall,
Whether he was pushed off, shoved without
Anybody asking him, "Are you ready to go?"—
Whether he said, "I've been an egg long enough,
And it's time for me to take a tumble"—
Whether it was just an accident and other eggs
Looking on said, "He was a good egg and we're sorry,"
Or, "He was a bad egg and it's just as well"—
Whether this or that happened and *why*
The recorders of Humpty have not told us.
He fell off a wall and that was the end.
Your guess is as good as the next one on the why of it.

He may never have sat on a wall before.
He may have been lifted onto the wall by other eggs
Laughing, "We shall give this egg a great fame."
He looked from the wall to the gravel far down.
He became dizzy thinking how high up he was
And the high cost of having fame, of listening
To the murmur far below of many little eggs
Repeating, "We shall give this egg a great fame."
From being dizzy he changed to being lonely.
He kept saying, "Jesus, it's cold up here,
Why was I lifted up here to be alone
And no other egg for me to say to 'how cold,
How far, how lonely, it is up here'?"
He either fell off because he wanted to,
Dropping down headfirst calling "Here goes!"
Or he was dizzy, cold, lonely, and found himself
Falling before he could do anything about it.

—From Two Commentaries on Humpty Dumpty[29]
by Carl Sandburg

Brothers Dalziel — *National Nursery Rhymes and Nursery Songs*, 1870

Mardi Gras Costume: Courtesy of the Atlanta Toy Museum

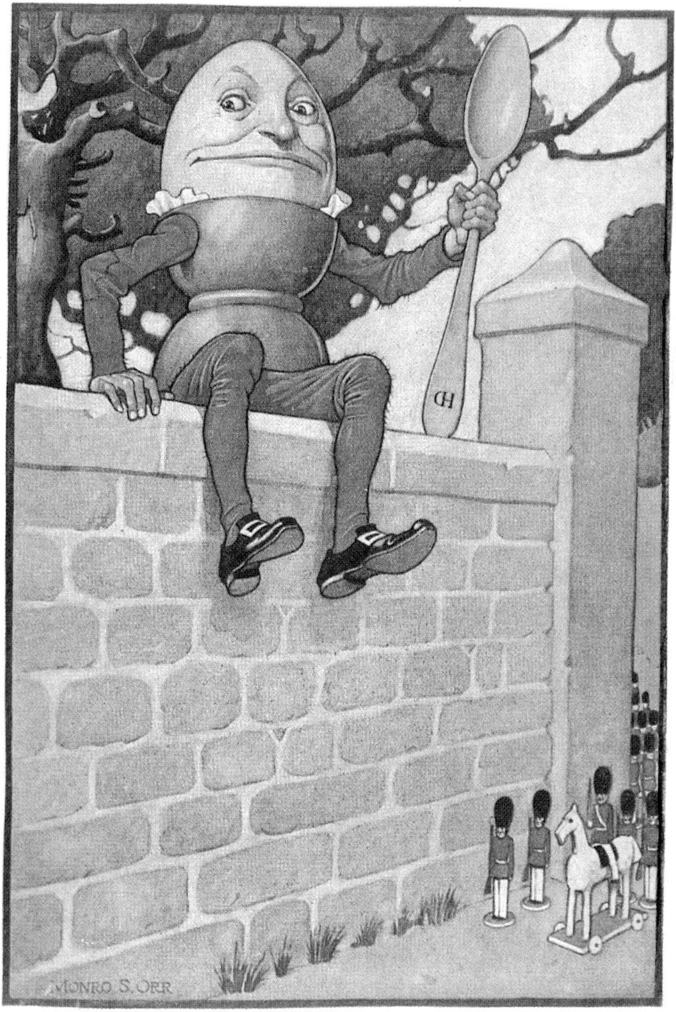
MONRO S. ORR
HD

Munro Orr — *Mother Goose*, 1915

Humpty Dumpty sat on a wall;

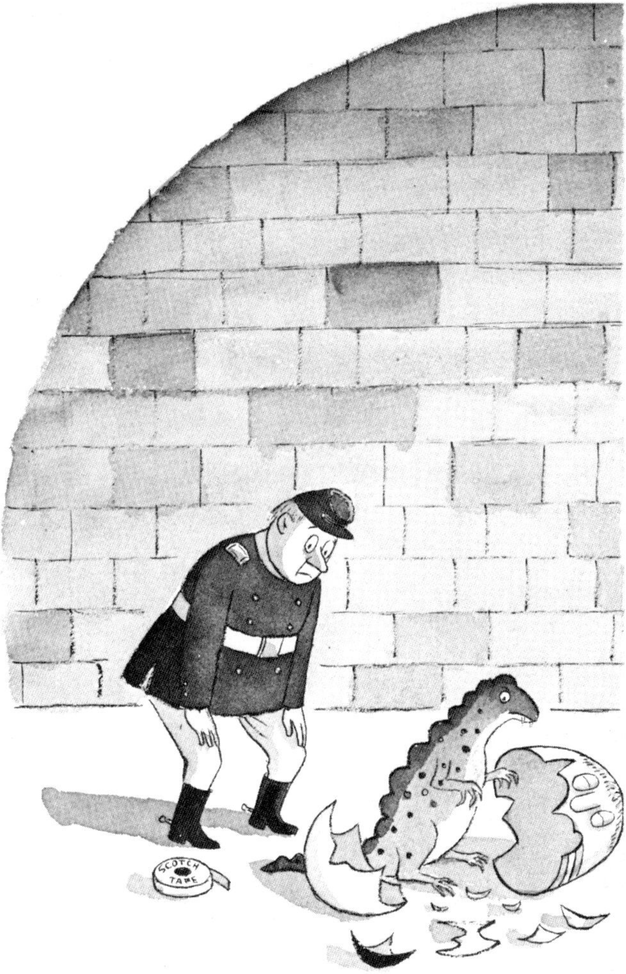
SCOTCH
TAPE

Humpty Dumpty had a great fall.

Charles Addams — *The Charles Addams Mother Goose*, 1967

Harry Otis Kennedy — *Old Mother Hubbard: Rhymes and Jingles With New Pictures*, 1902

Charles Folkard — *The Land of Nursery Rhyme*, 1932

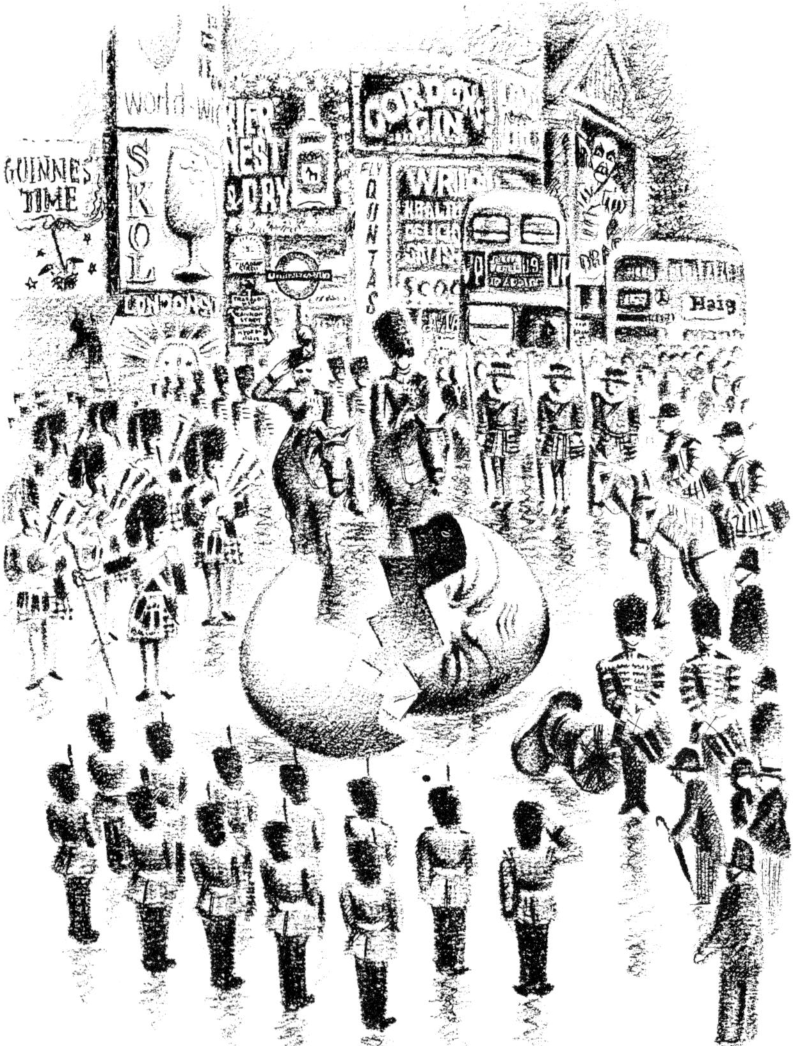
GUINNES' TIME
SKOL
Haig

ハンプティ・ダンプティ　へいにすわった
ハンプティ・ダンプティ　ころがりおちた
おうさまのおうまをみんな　あつめても
おうさまのけらいをみんな　あつめても
ハンプティを　もとにはもどせない

※なぞなぞ＝卵

Seiichi Horiuchi — *Mother Goose No Uta* Vol. 1, 1975

71

HUMPTY DUMPTY

Humpty Dumpty sat on a wall,
Humpty Dumpty had a great fall;
All the King's horses, and all the
    King's men
Cannot put Humpty Dumpty together
    again.

HUMPTY DUMPTY

Humpty Dumpty sat on a wall,
Humpty Dumpty had a great fall;
All the King's horses, and all the
    King's men
Cannot put Humpty Dumpty together
    again.

Blanche Fisher Wright — *The Real Mother Goose*, 1944

Klumpe Dumpe.

Klumpe Dumpe sad paa en tynd, tynd Gren,
Klumpe Dumpe faldt ned paa en stor,
                                    stor Sten.
Alle Kongens Penge og alle Kongens Mænd
sætter ikke Klumpe Dumpe sammen igen.

Sigurd Wandel — *Sommersang Og Venterleg*, 1900

Maxfield Parrish — *Mother Goose in Prose*, 1897

Brian Wildsmith — *Brian Wildsmith's Mother Goose*, 1965

Raymond Briggs — *Ring-a-Ring O'Roses*, 1962

REFERENCES

Baker, George Barr, Chappell, George C. and Herford, Oliver. *Mother's Geese*. pictured by T. Gilbert White. New York: Dodd, Mead & Co., 1906. (20)

Baring-Gould, William S. and Baring-Gould, Ceil. *The Annotated Mother Goose*. New York: Clarkson N. Potter, 1962.

Bett, Henry. *Nursery Rhymes and Tales: Their Origin and History*. New York: Henry Holt, & Co., 1924. (9)

Booth, Oliver. *Old Nursery Rhymes Dug Up at the Pyramids*. New York: H.M. Caldwell, n.d. (18)

Carroll, Lewis. *Through the Looking Glass*. 1871. (14)

Chappell, George C. See Baker, George Barr.

Denslow, W.W. *Mother Goose in Prose*. New York: Bounty Books, 1897. (17)

Eckenstein, Lina. *Comparative Studies in Nursery Rhymes*. London: Duckworth & Co., 1911 c1906. (13)

Greene, Douglas G. and Hearn, Michael Patrick. *W.W. Denslow*. Central Michigan University Press, 1976. (25)

Hackett, Earle. See Lear, John.

Harrowven, Jean. *The Origins of Rhymes, Songs and Sayings*. New Publications/Dufour Editions, 1977. (1)

Hopkins, Lee Bennett. *Books Are By People*. New York: Citation Press, 1969. (24, 27)

Lear, John. "The Ecologic of Nursery Rhymes." *Saturday Review*. November 6, 1971. (21)

Ludwig, Coy. *Maxfield Parrish*. New York: Watson-Guptill, 1973. (22)

MacDougall, James B. *The Real Mother Goose: The Reality Behind the Rhymes*. Toronto: The Ryerson Press, 1940.

Martin, Gardner. *The Annotated Alice*. New York: Bramhall House, 1960. (15)

Muir, Percy. *English Children's Books: 1600 to 1900*. New York: Frederick A. Praeger, 1954. (11)

Opie, Iona and Peter. *Oxford Dictionary of Nursery Rhymes*. London: Oxford, 1951. (8, 10)

Opie, Iona and Peter. *The Puffin Book of Nursery Rhymes*. Middlesex, England: Penguin Books, 1963. (7)

Opperman, D.J. *Kleuter-Verseboek*. Johannesburg: Nasionale Boekhandel Beperk, 1957. (26)

Pellowski, Anne. *The World of Children's Literature*. New York: Bowker, 1968. (23)

Sandburg, Carl. *Breathing Tokens*. New York: Harcourt, Brace and Jovanovich, 1978. (29)

Smith, Anna Marion. "Mother Goose Continued." *St. Nicholas*. January, 1907. (19)

Stevens, Albert Mason. *The Nursery Rhyme: Remnant of Popular Protest*. Lawrence, Kansas: Coronado Press, 1968. (2,3)

Taylor, Archer. *English Riddles From Oral Tradition*. Berkeley: University of California Press, 1951. (4, 5, 6)

Thomas, Katherine Elwes. *The Real Personages of Mother Goose*. Boston: Lothrop, 1930.

Thwaite, M.F. *From Primer to Pleasure*. London: The Library Association, 1963. (12)

Tobias, Tobi. *Isamu Noguchi: The Life of a Sculptor*. New York: Crowell, 1974. (28)

Walsh, Thomas. *Selected Poems of Thomas Walsh*. New York: Dial Press, 1930. (16)

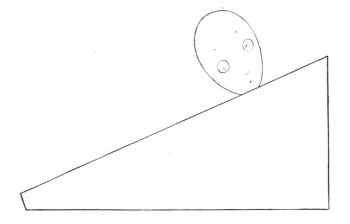

Thanks to those who aided in the research:
Childhood in Poetry Collection (Florida State University); Cooperative Children's Book Center (Madison, WI); Denmarks Paedagogiske Biblioteck (Kobenhavn); Fundacao Nacional Do Livro Infantil E Juvenil (Rio De Janeiro); Harvard Library; Institute for the Intellectual Development of Children and Young Adults (Tehran, Iran); Japanese Board on Books for Young People (Tokyo); The Jersusalem, Mayer Central Library (Israel); La Joie Par Les Livres (Paris); Kerlan Collection/University of Minnesota; Lexington Public Library (Lexington, KY); Library of Congress; San Diego Public Library; The Soviet Union National Section of IBBY (Moscow); Svenska Barnboksinstitutet (Stockholm); Text Book Centre Limited (Nairobi, Kenya); The USSR State Library (Moscow); United States Committee for UNICEF (New York); University of Chicago; University of Colorado; University of Kentucky; University of Michigan; University of Oregon; University of Wisconsin-Eau Claire; Wayne State University.

Willy Pogany — *Willy Pogany's Mother Goose*, 1928